FADO

FADO

NUNO ALMEIDA

LUC GODONOU DOSSOU

Édition : BoD – Books on Demand, info@bod.fr
Impression : BoD – Books on Demand,
In de Tarpen 42, Norderstedt (Allemagne)
Impression à la demande
ISBN: 978-2-3224-4381-9
Dépôt légal : Août 2022

Contents:

PROLOGUE

In Lisbon, every Saturday night, the most popular and trendiest club in the city hosts an exceptional evening that everyone dreams of being invited to.

It is as much a musical than a social gathering where two audiences that everything opposes meet and tame each other: the middle class living within the city walls and the bad boys coming from the ghetto. The man behind this success is called Miguel. This young label director signs young artists and DJs coming straight from the underprivileged suburbs.

Around one am, the crowd rushes to the entrance of the club but not everyone will be able to enter, only the most interesting people will be admitted. Miguel takes care of welcoming the VIPs and charges everyone who is not on the guest list. As he is the producer of the evening, he receives fifty percent of entrance fees and he is already excited thinking of the small fortune he will make. At the back of the club, his right hand man stationed in the dark ensures that the club owner does not bring in any friend through the emergency door for free. Miguel is smart, cunning, he knows all the managers' tricks and is wary of them.

Fortunately, the evening ends uneventfully and without bloodshed. The young man goes to the boss's office to receive his share for the evening. The latter hands him a less than thick wad of banknotes. Miguel is suspicious, he knows some cash is missing. He recounts under the eyes of the boss and his guard dog as they begin to sweat. The security guard stands close to the boss, ready for all eventualities but especially for the worst.

Miguel is well known in the middle of the night; his tough reputation is well established. The count is not right, of course, but the young entrepreneur remains calm. He knows what he has to do in this kind of situation. He targets the security guard first, staring at him.

- You, he says, pointing at him. Let us chat for two minutes.

The person he is pointing to does not move, the director begins to shake.

- If you don't get out of here right away, I promise you I'll go visit your little family and especially your brats. They're still going to school downtown, right?

A bead of sweat forms on the man's forehead, he clenches his jaw but chooses to disobey his superior at the risk of losing his job. Even if Miguel is not very strong, he has an aura about him. He ends up leaving under the frightened eyes of his boss who is silently begging him to stay. The threat often works. The young man approaches the director with a threatening look. From his belt, he pulls out a hidden knife, a small penknife seemingly harmless but terribly sharp. His most faithful companion, he always keeps it on him, just in case. He creeps up to the director, sitting in his chair, shaking and sweating profusely. In a split second, he places the small knife under the mingy man's greasy throat as he begins to squeal like a helpless animal. Miguel calms him down by pressing the knife a little harder on his throat. He doesn't need to do anything else, the man gives in.

- Take it, take everything! begs the manager, pointing to the rest of the money.

Miguel is satisfied, he got what he wanted. A broad smile curls up on his face as he prepares to head home and celebrate this victory. Beyond the cultural mix he instilled, the young director is a real business shark. He had been terribly lacking money in his life and he will not let anyone take what is his due. But Miguel forgets one thing: Humiliation, like revenge, is a double-edged sword. And such behaviour, more often than not, comes with consequences…

CHAPTER 1

A chilly August evening. Nelson had just finished his tour, he shivered as he got back on his red scooter. On his way home, he was daydreaming about music. He knew what he would do as soon as he got home: compose. Tonight, he wouldn't join the gang that hung around the towers, he was tired of being teased by them. Even though he knew they weren't doing it out of wickedness, he couldn't help but compare himself to Miguel, his brother, the kingpin, the prodigy. While he sold soft pizzas and dreamed of music, his brother ran one of the biggest music labels in the area, and it was he who provided the income that allowed them both to survive. Tonight he was on a big spree: a night out at the most upscale nightclub in town, and Miguel had a front row seat. Of course, when he got home, he would be sure to brag about how much money he had made. His brother was greedy, cunning and vicious. He represented a threat to the competition, and did not hesitate to get his hands dirty to get what he wanted, besides, his reputation tended to precede him: he was feared and respected. Money was his second family, or truth be told, I even think it was his first. And that made all the difference. They had truly grown since leaving Cape Verde and had gradually drifted apart, as sometimes it happens in life.

After a 20-minute drive, he arrived home. His brother earned a good living, but that did not prevent him from living in the least wealthy part of the suburbs. Their house was a small shack with shaky walls and a roof that was missing a few tiles. They had ended up getting used to living in this slum that had kept the smells and shadows of their childhood. Nelson parked his delivery scooter at the back, making as little noise as possible. All he wanted to do was go up to his room to indulge in his favourite activity without attracting any attention. But Miguel was already there, waiting for him, slumped on the couch.

- Nel! I was waiting for you. I made so much money tonight!

He straightened himself and stood up. A wide smile appeared on his tanned face.

- How much? Nelson asked, indifferent.

- Look at that! He waved the wad of cash under the boy's nose. Enough to not worry about money for a while. And to think that I almost got screwed, they tried to screw me over, these motherfuckers!

As usual, Nelson thought, rolling his eyes. Miguel cut the bundle in half and threw it on the table.

- Take it, treat yourself.

This sentence was full of innuendo but Nelson managed to stifle his annoyance and took the money. He thanked his brother and then went up to his room, which he double-locked. Tonight, he wanted to write a song about his love for music and no one was allowed to come and disturb him. Kizomba had been his favourite musical genre since childhood and it fit perfectly into Portugal's landscape and traditions. He had been spoon fed Afro music since childhood and it had been carrying him ever since. It made him dream of a new life, far from the ghetto. Of a simple and peaceful life centered by only one thing: his love of music. Nothing mattered to him anymore. But one day that dream would become reality and he would finally be happy and fulfilled. Nelson had promised himself that he would leave as soon as the opportunity arose, without looking back, leaving behind him this life that he hated a little more each day. A bluish butterfly came to rest on the sill of his window, flapping its wings. Nelson noticed it and thought that sometimes life did show us beautiful things. Then he lost himself again to the music.

CHAPTER 2

The young boy raced down the stairs, almost tripping. He had forgotten to wake up this morning and was late for work. Out of the corner of his eye, he noticed that Miguel had remained on the sofa and that a half-naked young woman had joined him during the night. Empty beer bottles were scattered all over the place, along with a few clothes and still-lit cigarettes. A strong cannabis smell was floating through the air. He violently slammed the door behind him to express his anger and got on his scooter. Lateness had been his best friend lately, but his boss had made it very clear: no more being late or he would be fired. And Nelson could not lose that job, that was the only thing that would get him out of that hell hole. Suddenly he braked abruptly. A police car appeared around the corner. Those parasites were always there, watching for the slightest gesture, the slightest misstep of people of the same species as Nelson. That's what they called them to hide their racism, people of the same species, different from their own species, inferior. Whenever they got the chance, they would harass the local youth. They drove closely by Nelson, and Nelson prayed they would not arrest him. His prayers were heard, they drove past him slowly, and in what seemed like a never-ending moment, glared suspiciously at him, then went on to continue patrolling. Relieved, he rushed off again, there was no way he would be late again!

It had been a busy day, Nelson was exhausted. But he had one last order to deliver before going home and it was his biggest of the day. He drove to the given address and the closer he got to his destination, the more the surroundings were changing. The houses were bigger and more luxurious. Soon enough, he arrived in front of a huge house lit up by several beams of light emanating from a British green lawn. He stopped to admire it. One day, he would have a similar house. He walked towards the sturdy, bright red, wooden door, his arms loaded with a dozen piping hot pizzas. He managed to knock on the door. He recognized immediately the man with delicate features who opened the door.

- Hello, I'm the delivery guy. I'm bringing you your order, Nelson said with a laugh.

- Nelson! said loudly the man with a big smile. Glad to see you my boy!

He invited the young boy in. In the background, Afro music was playing.

- You can drop off the pizzas here, he said pointing to a table. I'll be back, I'll go get your money.

As Nelson observed the people surrounding him, he realized that all the guests were white. The host of the evening returned with a few bills.

- I'm sorry but I only have this on hand, he

says, waving the bills and scratching the back of his head. May I offer you a drink to pay for the rest? The theme of this private event is music and I seem to recall it being your thing...

This sneaky man was trying to get free pizzas and appease the young man. Although he seemed very friendly, Ricardo was no fool, he knew how to win people over and obtain favours from them. But Nelson could not come back with half the money, especially for such a big order.

- Sorry Ricardo, but you have to pay for the entire order. Otherwise I will have to take back the unpaid pizzas.

- Alright, alright, fine! You're tough on business, he said, pouting.

He reached into his pockets, disappointed that he had not succeeded in convincing him, and pulled out more bank notes that he handed to Nelson. The latter recounted everything.

- It's good for me, thank you. I have to go, have fun!

He cast one last look around him, knowing that, deep down, he would have liked to be among the guests.

- Hey man, my offer for a drink still stands, can I show you around? Ricardo said seeing the young man's disappointed look.

Not far from them, Veronica, an acquaintance of Nelson's, has recognized him and is watching them talk. She is a regular at Miguel's parties and often hears him talking about his little brother, who is only good at daydreaming. Because of the family resemblance, she thought she saw Miguel from afar, for whom she has a secret crush. She ends up joining them, a glass of champagne in her hand.

- What are you doing here, Nel? she nicely asked.

It took Nelson some time to recognize the young woman. He had only seen her a few times alongside her brother.

- Veronica, I'm glad to see you, it's been a while!

- You know each other? asked Ricardo, surprised.

- We know each other indirectly, explained

Veronica. His brother organizes parties and I've met Nelson a few times. But tell me Nel', it's a fact that we don't see you hanging around with your brother as much.

- Yes, I found a job as a delivery man so I don't really have time to accompany him to his parties anymore.

And I don't want to either, he thought.

- Well, since you know two each other, let's all have a drink together! Nelson, you can no longer say no!

As the young man was once again going to decline the offer, Veronica motioned to one of her friends to join them. Nelson turned around to greet the young woman walking towards them and suddenly stopped. Before him stood an angel in an evening dress. Something inside him screamed in glee...what a wonderful person!!! But still he, barely, managed to remain stoic.

- Ricardo, Nel', this is Ana, she's a friend of mine from music school.

Ana gave them a shy wave. Nelson was mesmerized by her beauty. Her dazzling blond hair made her small blue almond eyes stand out and her dress, a magnificent royal blue, contrasted with her white skin. His heart was pounding. A young man in a tuxedo appeared behind her and put his hands on her shoulders. The girl frowned.

- Hello, I'm Jorge, nice to meet you.

He shook both men's hands and kissed Veronica's. He, too, looked very elegant in a tuxedo that matched Ana's dress, but something in his voice rang false. He immediately grabbed her arm as if to showcase how close they were, which slightly annoyed Nelson. Ricardo invited them to smoke some weed in the cool air of the balcony. The small group began talking. Ana and Nelson ended up isolating themselves from the group and started discussing all styles of music. The young man was delighted, he felt like a fish in water. For once, people were not making fun of him and he was able to express himself freely about his passion. From where he was standing, Jorge could not help but cast furtive glances in their direction. He did not appreciate at all their closeness and how these two were starting to bond. Ana was his, she was his betrothed. He had planned his whole life around her and he would not let anyone jeopardize their future together.

- Hey Nelson, do you know where we can get some weed? Real, good stuff, not green tea! Ricardo asked, a bit tipsy.

- It's true, if you have a good tip, you can share it with us! Veronica add.

- Yeah, I know a guy. He's my brother's supplier. I can get some from him if you want.

- That would be great, and since you like music so much, you should come to the music school, we have a great singing teacher. Tomorrow, we have a class with him at the end of the afternoon, you will give us the weed then.

- That way, you can meet the Professor, he is really talented! Ana cheerfully exclaimed.

Seeing her joy and eagerness, Nelson could not refuse this offer. After all, he would have given anything to see her again. Suddenly he saw another blue butterfly and wondered if it was the same as the day before. The butterfly twirled for a moment in front of his eyes and then went away carried by the wind.

CHAPTER 3

Nelson had been waiting for this moment all day long. He was eager to see Ana again and to attend this famous Professor's course that the two girls had been praising the merits of. It would be a first for him and he hoped not to be disappointed with this whole venture. He was so excited that he almost forgot to go buy the weed from his brother's supplier. He went to the sale meetup, bought a small package and sped towards the city centre where the music school was located. Veronica and

Ana were already waiting for him in the parking lot. From a distance he recognized Ana's shiny hair, which she had carefully pulled back into a high ponytail. No sooner had he cut the engine than Veronica was on him, demanding her order. He handed her the little odorant package and she gave him some money in return.

- Class starts in a few minutes, said the latter. Come on, we shouldn't be late. The Professor is a rather strict man even if he doesn't look that way at first.

Together they headed into the building. Nelson felt surprisingly comfortable. In front of the classroom door, a well-dressed man wearing round glasses was inviting the students in. Ana nudged Nelson lightly.

"It's the Professor," she whispered in his ear.

Nelson could not help but notice her delicate scent. It was the kind of perfume that could turn a man into a slave, a disciple, the kind that makes you hate every other scents, as if the whole world were nothing more than a gigantic trashcan…it was undoubtedly the sweetest and nicest fragrance he had smelled in his entire life.

- Hello girls and hello young man, said the Professor arching an eyebrow. I think I haven't seen you in here before.

Ana did not let Nelson say a single word.

- Hello Sir, this is Nelson, he is a friend of mine. He would like to attend your class, he is both a singer and a composer.

- You don't say, well young man, welcome! Seeing new faces in my class is always a pleasure. I am the teacher in charge of the music lessons, I hope you will enjoy this one. But first tell me, what do you usually like to sing?

- It is a pleasure for me Sir to have the opportunity to attend one of your classes, Nelson replied as politely as possible. I really like Kizomba.

- Very well, I hope my lesson won't disappoint you.

The four of them shared a smile and walked into the classroom. Ana saved a seat for Nelson next to her, much to his delight. Even though they only had met each other last night, she was enjoying his company more and more which each passing minute. His simplicity and his kindness were the two qualities she had first noticed in the young man. She was delighted to share this moment with him. She discreetly observed Nelson during the lesson, he was displaying a radiant smile and looked like the happiest man in the world. She found him very handsome, his dark skin and full lips gave him a peculiar charm. His robust physique was a testimony that life had not been easy on hi; a few tattoos on his arms made him look like a cute bad boy. Although Jorge was never far from her, Ana allowed her thoughts to wander, after all, her mind was still a free place. Jorge was not a bad person but he tended to be overbearing. He came from a good family, like Ana, was a university student, like Ana, was invited to all kinds of parties, like Ana. He was always there and she could not take it anymore! Even his father idolized the boy, for him he was the perfect son-in-law, but neither of them had ever asked the young girl if agreed. Indeed, she pictured a completely different life for herself, but no one knew about it and even worse, nobody cared about it.

CHAPTER 4

That night, Nelson decided to go spend some time with the group he had not been hanging out with for a long time. He felt calm and ready to put up with all their teasing. The afternoon class had been a moment of pure enlightenment. Not only had he had fun like a child in an amusement park, but it had also confirmed all of his plans. And of course there was also Ana. Having her net to him for a whole hour and sharing this moment with her had provided him with the kind of happiness he would not have allowed himself to dream of. At times, he caught her looking discreetly in his direction. He reckoned she was feeling the same way, that she too had experienced this "love at first sight". And to think I believed I could only love music… he thought. For the first time ever, someone had managed to almost outshine music. Still, music remained his first love. He would only tell his brother about it if absolutely necessary. Miguel did not need to know everything about his life and even less about his plans.

As usual, his friends were hanging around in the parking lot of the housing complex, drinking beers and teasing each other. When they noticed the young man approaching, they could not help but point out his numerous absences. He explained that it was due to a heavy workload. One of his friends offered him a joint which he hastily took, along with a lukewarm beer. Looking around, watching his friends while thinking of Ana, Nelson wondered if leaving this place was not too drastic a decision. After all, the ghetto had been his home for his whole life, he had had his first kiss right here and he had spent thousands of hours there just hanging around with his friends. Even though life had been tough, he still felt a sort of nostalgia for this place. Was Ana the reason behind it? Maybe. Since their meeting, she had been haunting his every thought. He, who used to not believe in love at first sight... Tomorrow, he would see her again, and the next day too, as well as the day after and then every day when he would have the opportunity to go to music school. He would attend all the classes, both for his love of music and to see Ana, a little bit more to see Ana. She was glad he was here with her, she had told him. Moreover, the Professor, who greatly appreciated Nelson and his innate talent for music, had invited him to the school's annual performance during which he had planned to reveal the name of the most brilliant student in his classes. He would be one of the only black person amongst white people but it didn't matter to him, people were believing in him for the very first time and he intended to show everyone his talent as a singer. He was planning on inviting his brother to show him the power of music, to prove to him that he too could be successful, without violence and without roguery. At the exact moment the Professor invited him to the event, he instantly knew what music he would sing: a love song, dedicated to all lovers of traditional Portuguese music and, of course, to Ana. Even though he was not sure the Professor would choose him, he had to prepare himself and he was going to give everything he had during the next few classes.

It would be his chance, an unexpected opportunity, the stepping-stone to a better life. Just thinking about it, Nelson was almost bursting with joy.

The only obstacle that stood in his way was Jorge, the boy from a good family, the pretentious prick. Without knowing why, he did not trust him and his way of hovering over Ana, like a predator was not the least bit reassuring. Jorge had the bland face of people who never seem to understand anything, of people who look around the room for someone dumber than them but can never find anyone. Ana was usually beaming, but her face did frown when Jorge appeared at Ricardo's party. Nelson had felt that he had to be wary of him from their first meeting. He had felt his reprimanding gaze as he was talking to Ana that night. He wondered how Jorge would react if he found out that they were seeing each other every day at music school. Come to think of it, he was better off ignoring that fact.

CHAPTER 5

The more music lessons passed, the more Nelson's brilliance revealed itself for all of his classmates to witness. His performances were impressive, full of emotion without sacrificing any of the precision. The Professor ended up taking him under his wing. He offered him the possibility to attend classes for free. Of course, he had asked for complete discretion regarding this matter as to avoid any problems. Nelson was delighted, and even though he had chosen to politely refuse the offer at first, he finally accepted. An opportunity like this would not present itself twice, especially for such a prestigious music school. In addition to this good news, he had been invited to the school's annual representation, where the Professor would announce the best student in his class. He hoped it would be him, but according to Ana, there was no doubt about it. The pair had grown very close, spending most of their time together under the inquisitive gaze of Jorge, who was now following Ana everywhere, even to her university when Nelson was not around. At first glance, they seemed like the best of friends, but everyone except Jorge knew that what was happening between those two was deeper than friendship. They talked, laughed, teased each other and often shared a good joint after music lessons to debrief. Nelson had never felt something so real for a girl. He had already been in love of course, but it had only been fleeting crushes. He had given up on love altogether, convincing himself that his great love was and would always be music. Nowadays, he was not so sure of it anymore. Ana was one of the reasons that had made him accept to follow the Professor's music lessons for free. Spending those few hours every day next to her her while learning music was a moment of pure ecstasy for him. He loved the young girl with all his heart and dreamed of spending his nights with her since their very first meeting.

Ana had something important to do and had asked Nelson to accompany her. This day had been very strange, he had found his friend slightly absentminded, as if her mind was elsewhere. She had remained pensive and silent throughout the lesson and Nelson wondered what was happening with her. The talkative and excited young girl had been replaced by a completely different person. He was worried and stressed out, thinking her behaviour was somehow his fault; and to make matters worse, Ana would not tell him what was going on and where she was planning to take him. The truth behind her vacant stares was that it had been a year to the day that her mother had passed out, losing her battle to a fatal cancer. She remembered like it was yesterday the heart-breaking goodbyes. The woman she had known to be radiant and full of determination had become a fragile person with pale skin and dull eyes that she could not look at without crying. She often tried to push past those painful memories to reminisce about a time before the cancer, when it was all laughter and songs. As they got closer to the cemetery, Nelson finally understood what was bothering Ana and stopped asking her questions. When he found himself in front of the grave and read the name on the white stone, he stiffened. This carved pebble reminded him of old painful memories that he had preferred to bury deep inside of him. He said nothing and just placed his hand on Ana's back for support. Even if he did not really understand why she had brought him here, he was happy to be one of the person she chose to trust. On the way back, Ana remained silent while a few tears rolled out of her eyes. She finally said a few words.

- Thanks for coming with me today, I'm usually alone, she said softly.

- No problem, answered Nelson tenderly. But isn't your father coming with you?

- No, he doesn't like this kind of place. I think it's still too hard for him to accept the death of his wife.

- It's understandable, it's not an easy thing to cope with, especially when it's such an important person.

- Mmh yes, I guess.

- And Jorge, he's never come with you?

This stalker, he thought.

- No, I don't want him to come here. My mother didn't like him very much and he didn't like her either. I don't want him to sully her memory. You, I knew you would understand.

She offered him a smile, her first one of the day.

- That I would understand because both my parents are dead?

Nelson had briefly brought up the subject one evening while they were having a beer. He did not really remember their death since he was so young, the only thing he truly remembered was the terrifying hurricane that took their lives in Cape Verde.

- Yes, but also because you're a sensitive and caring person, Nel' and that's what I like about you. I know you are honest and that I can trust you. I feel good with you; I feel like I can be myself around you.

The young boy did not know what to say. Ana suddenly stopped walking.

- What are you doing? he asked, facing her.

The girl threw herself into his arms and burst into tears. The anniversary of her mother's death had something to do with it, but it was more than that. Nelson hugged her tight, seeing her in this state broke his heart. The only thing he could say was: I'm sorry Ana. At that moment, another blue butterfly or maybe it was the same one, brushed against him then continued on its way, twirling. Surprising, all these blue butterflies…he thought.

CHAPTER 6

The young boy was still quite upset after events of the past day. Ana had never told him anything about her mother up until yesterday and now he finally understood why. But on the other hand, it had brought them even closer and he was happy about that. Hugging Ana had been very pleasant and had confirmed that he did in fact really love her. He decided to write her a love song that he would sing at the school's annual performance, still hoping to be chosen by the Professor. His music would speak of love, death, travel, dreams and desires. He dreamed of enchanting his audience, moving them to tears. It would be his first appearance on stage and he simply had to make a grand impression. Ana was the muse that would help him sublimate his music. He crumpled up the piece of paper on which he had started writing the song he had originally planned for the performance. Now, he intended to create a perfect work of art. He spent hours on end writing and rewriting until the harmony between the words and the notes finally gave him a sense of satisfaction. That was his absolute best work, now it was up to the public to judge him.

After finishing his masterpiece, Nelson decided to go see Ana, directly at her house, but he had something to do first. While he was writing, he had realized that his desire to escape the shady suburbs where he had grown up had vanished. With Ana by his side, he was fulfilled and if she wanted to stay, he would stay too. He went to his boss, Tonio who ran the pizza place and quit. He no longer needed this job, from now on, he had everything he needed to be happy. He took to the road again on his scooter, with a lighter heart and it was not long before he arrived to his beloved's house. She was waiting for him in front of her grand and imposing home. No sooner had they entered than he handed her his song to read and carefully watched all the emotions displayed on her face.

- You're the one who inspired me for this piece, I hope you don't mind…

- Not at all, it's lovely! On the contrary, it makes me happy… And if music doesn't suit you, you can always become a poet! she said, laughing.

- If the Professor happens to choose me, this is the song I want to perform. You were my inspiration and it's one of the most beautiful songs I've ever written.

Ana blushed, Nelson smiled.

-Come on, let's have a drink, the young girl suggested.

He followed her to the kitchen. The house was huge but Ana seemed to be its only occupant.

- You're alone?

- Yes, my dad is at work, he will surely come back for the performance.

Anna shrugged. Although she seemed to show very little interest for her father, she still regretted the fact that they had grown apart since her mother's death. Nowadays, her father was nothing like the man he once was. All his cheerfulness and compassion were gone. He would rather dedicate his free time to business and making money than spending time with his daughter. It looked like, for him, his whole family had disappeared on that fateful date.

- Shall I show you my bedroom?

Nelson nodded, choking on a sip of his beer. The prospect of visiting the bedroom of such a beautiful creature made his legs a little shaky, a slight shake, barely noticeable. As he had expected, Ana her bedroom to be truly hers: both simple and pretty. On a white wooden console was a family photo, father on the left, mother on the right and his beautiful girl in the middle: a picture perfect family.

- It's your mother? Nelson asked, knowing the answer already.

- No, no, it's the cook, then she burst out

laughing.

- You look like her, you both have the same smile and the same eyes.

- Apple didn't fall too far from the tree!

- Ana, can I ask you a question?

- I'm listening.

- Why are you dating Jorge if you don't love him?

Nelson had hit a nerve. Ana tensed up and started playing with her hair as a reflex.

- You don't owe me an answer, you know. It's just that when he's around, you always act really different.

- I know. And I'm sorry about that. When my mother left, he was the only person who didn't treat me any differently. Between my father who refused to accept the reality of her death and people who would only talk to me about it or constantly ask me how I felt, I couldn't take it anymore! I felt comfortable around him because he continued to act as his usual self, as if nothing had happened. And I needed normalcy, to avoid overthinking. He was my rock for a while but soon, I understood that the reason he was acting the sae was simply because he didn't actually give a fuck that she wasn't there anymore and now I can't stand him anymore.

- I'm sorry we didn't know each other before, I wish I could have helped you back then.

- We met at the perfect time, believe me, she said, tenderly stroking his face. You and me, we really found each other.

He wanted to kiss and hug her but it was not the right time, it was still too soon. And he did not want to ruin this sweet moment.

- And what about you, did you come here after the hurricane?

- Yes, after my parents' death. But because I was so young, I don't actually remember them. It was Miguel who took it the hardest. Our grandmother welcomed us here afterwards, orphans and homeless. All I remember is music; my mother used to sing all the time, I remember her voice more than her face.

- And I imagine it was hard for your brother?

- Yes, I remember him spending most of his time getting into fights and then one day he understood that fighting could actually pay off and he started making money. We had already drifted apart, we almost became total strangers. But I have to admit, he is the only reason we managed to get by since the death of our grandmother. I got my mother's sensibility, he got our father's arrogance of those who know what they want and are not afraid to proclaim it to the world. It makes me sad to see him addicted to money, that's the only thing that matters to him now. But I still admire his courage to go after what he wants and I'm jealous of his freedom.

A comfortable silence settled, the two young people were deep in their thoughts. In fact, both their misfortunes were quite similar, but today they were their strength. Ana finally stood up and placed a kiss on Nelson's cheek. Secretly he planned to never washing that part of his face again...

Returning home that evening, the young boy thought back to their conversation and to Miguel, whom he found, once again, slouched on their shabby sofa and stoned out of his mind. He silently looked at him for a moment, and wondered why his brother always dressed the same. A beanie, a black sweater and a pair of jeans... always the same outfit during all those years, apart from the occasional evening suit. It was intriguing. He hesitated, then decided against inviting him to the performance. In response, his brother growled in his sleep. At least he would not regret not inviting him.

CHAPTER 7

The day of the annual performance had finally arrived, it was happening in just a few hours and Nelson was already on edge. After spending so much time preparing, all these lessons, these rehearsals, and all the questionings with Ana, he was ready to show the world the extent of his talent and of his unconditional love for music. In the room, students' families were getting restless, hoping that their child would be the lucky one. Once again, the young boy felt alone and out of place: most of the people around him were white.

He had hoped to see a familiar face in the audience to support him, his brother perhaps, but he had not shown much interest in the event when he had finally decided to invite him. His chair was empty. Nelson took his place and soon Veronica joined him. Out of the corner of his eye, he looked at Ana: she was sitting next to her father, a tall, white, rigid man. This potbellied man had the curves of a man who had spent his time eating his success while despising the rest of the world. It is easier to climb the ladder when you are white. It is simply a fact… His face did not look very friendly at all, especially compared to his daughter's, which was radiating kindness.

The Professor appeared on stage and the whole room fell silent. Nelson's heart was pounding in his chest.

- Good evening everyone and thank you for coming, he started. Tonight is going to be an exceptional evening because, as you all know, I will announce this year's prodigy and offer him or her the opportunity to officially enter the world of music with my full support.

Acting as if he was about to announce an Academy Award winner, the Professor took out a small sealed beige envelope from the inner pocket of his tuxedo. The suspense was at its highest level. He gently opened the envelope and smiled as he read the card.

- Tonight, ladies and gentlemen, is an exceptional evening. You will discover in a few moments the revelation of this year… He paused as everyone held their breath in anticipation. Please give a proper triumph for my new prodigy: Nelson!

His heart exploded with pride while the room erupted in shouting and applause. When he got up to perform on stage, a few murmurs rose in the room. Going up on stage, he took a last look at the room. Miguel had officially chosen not come and someone had taken the opportunity to take his seat. Even if he was disappointed, he was not surprised. But it was not the time to think, it was the time to sing and show all these white and contemptuous rich people his immense talent. Nelson took a deep breath and sang like never before the beautiful song he had written for Ana. With all his body and soul, he closed his eyes and pushed his voice to the limit.

Beads of sweat ran down his face. He opened his eyes and saw Ana, in the middle of the crowd, with sparkling eyes and a dazzling smile, she knew he was singing for her. Backstage, the Professor was the proudest man in the world, no one could have performed better than Nelson. He sang perfectly, the notes, the sounds, everything was synchronized and created a perfect harmony. The melody was beautiful and sweet and his deep voice gave it a touch of manliness. The public was moved, some held their breath and others wiped away a tear, but all were amazed by the talent of the young man.

The melody stopped, Nelson opened his eyes and thunderous applause rang out. The cheers were so loud he could hear them echoing in his chest. He could not help but smile and his eyes sparkled. The Professor came to thank him, gave him a hug and whispered in his ear: Congratulations, it was wonderful!

After the show had ended, Nelson went to find Ana. She was still in shock.

- Did you like it? the boy tenderly asked.

- Of course I liked it, it was beautiful! I hope

you will sing it to me again...

Her small blue eyes were sparkling with emotion. Nelson took her in his arms. The girl's father joined them. It was the first time they met face to face. Understanding that the friend his daughter was always talking about was nothing but a miserable black kid from the slums, Paolo stiffened, looking disdainful. Nelson did possess a certain musical talent but that did not he mean he belonged with his daughter, they belonged to different worlds, different species. He decided to go say hello anyway, out of mere politeness. From Nelson's point of view, he thought that Ana's father did not appreciate him. His handshake was strong, as if he wanted to impress him. His gaze, cold and conceited, did not hide his true feelings. Nelson had images racing through his mind, and he thought to himself that this man had never seduced anyone and that he was bitter because he had had to buy everything in life, even love. Fortunately, Ana was there to interrupt this tense moment. She dragged Nelson to the small buffet put up by the school to lighten his mood.

- Don't pay attention to my father, she said

raising her eyebrows. He is always like that, with everyone, the only one who has ever been good enough for him is Jorge.

Although Nelson had gone to see Ana at her house a few times, he had not yet had the opportunity to meet Paolo, her father. He was always away on business trips and was hardly ever at home. Although the girl assured him that this was her father's nature, Nelson was not convinced. This guy sounded like he was a racist to his very core. It was clear to Nelson when he saw how Paolo was looking at the few other dark-skinned people in the room and his eyes were screaming what he could not say: these people do not belong here.

To make matter worse, Jorge showed up. He was determined to not give Nelson any chance. He was quick to inform Paolo that his daughter was hanging out more and more with this young black man who was taking advantage of people's charity to attend music lessons for free. Of course, after these revelations, her father got into a rage. That his daughter was friends with a black man was one thing, but that this friend was allowed to attend these overpriced classes for free was inconceivable, unfair even! He had to have a serious talk with the boy, but this was neither the time nor the place, Ana would resent him forever. He would wait for a proper time and he would deliver a proper blow. A single sentence would be enough to destroy his new and upcoming career as a musician. He was going to make him regret ever coming on his turf!

CHAPTER 8

The performance was over and the room began slowly emptying. Paolo waited and waited until everyone had gone home. Out of the corner of his eye, he watched the comings and goings of the Professor who was greeting the students that were leaving and when he too was about to leave, he went up to him to block his way and did not hesitate to clearly express what was on his mind.

- Professor, I need to talk to you! he said, gritting his teeth.

- Sure thing! You are Ana's dad, right?

- Yes, he said harshly.

- Your daughter is one of my best students, she is studious and persistent! She is attentive, determined and full of…

Paolo cut him off. He wasn't there to listen to praises about his daughter.

- Professor, I find it simply unacceptable that you offer free lessons to a black man from the outskirts of town, while everyone else has to pay for your lessons!

The Professor did not expect this. His benevolent expression disappeared. He had asked Ana and Nelson not to say anything about his offer but obviously word had travelled. He did not do it out of the kindness of his heart as everyone thought, but rather out of spite. All the students he had welcomed into his classroom were certainly talented, but no one had impressed him quite as much as Nelson had. Nobody. And he was not going to let a disgruntled, musically illiterate parent ruin this for him. Especially if he was racist.

- Listen sir, he said calmly. This young boy is

extremely talented, he is passionate and creative. You have seen it yourself, if I chose to let him attend my classes for free, it is simply because I know that this opportunity will never come again and that I cannot bring myself to pass by his talent for a matter of a few cents.

- He may have talent but he doesn't belong here, I don't want him to come to this school anymore! It's not his world; do him a solid and send him back to his shack. I'm paying, that gives me the right to tell you what I think! If you keep teaching that foreigner, you can say goodbye to your school's good reputation!

The Professor remained unconcerned. The reputation of his school was beyond criticism. It was well known all over the world and could not be altered by a racist snob. Ana's father left the room, boiling with rage. He no longer had a choice. He had to go after Nelson directly. He needed an accomplice for his plan. Jorge would be the perfect man for this job, he did not like Nelson either and seeing him hovering around his future wife was driving him crazy. Paolo would not need to argue much to convince him. But Ana could not know anything, otherwise what was left of their family would be shattered forever. The girl hated the racist side of her father, she did not understand it. He saw these people as parasites, less than humans who swarmed on the outskirts of the city and fuelled drugs trades. They were getting more and more numerous, violent and cruel. Some even had the audacity to come all the way to the city centre for their delinquent activities. As proof: just a few days before, a nightclub owner had been stabbed for a mere few bucks. The police no longer scared them and it was rather quite the opposite. Paolo could not understand people like the Professor who helped and defended them. Was he the only one to see them for who they truly were? The only one who worried about his little girl every day? The mere thought of it was a torture! Someone had to do something about them and if the police were not going to do their job, then he did not mind getting his hands dirty for the sake of the city and for his daughter.

CHAPTER 9

Miguel felt bad for not coming to his brother's performance. On one hand, he was happy for Nelson, the fact that he was living his dream had transformed him: he was now a beaming and ambitious young man like Miguel had been when he had started out as a label manager. But on the other hand, he was worried that he was one of the only black people in the school, worried that he had fallen in love with a girl from a good family and worried that he had quit his job as a delivery boy. Nelson was his only family here, apart from his friends. His brother was his blood and even if he had been neglecting him, family was still family. Since leaving Cape Verde following the hurricane that killed both their parents, they had drifted apart from each other. They had fled with their grandmother and had taken refuge in the suburbs of Lisbon and had been surviving until today. Their very old grandmother had ended up dying too. Miguel had, therefore, taken on the role of a fatherly figure and this had affected their relationship. To make matters worse, he had been very busy with his label and had been neglecting Nelson. Eventually, they had become two strangers only talking to each other occasionally. What was even worse was that the state of their relationship did not seem to bother Nelson. Even if Miguel acted tough, he had a tender heart and he would have given his life for his little brother in a split second. The young man did not know why he suddenly felt so nostalgic, and last but not least, the big night at the club was weighing on him. Organizing it was a tremendous amount of work and the word on the street was that someone was coming for him. The front door opened behind him, startling him, causing him to spill his beer on the floor. He groaned, his little brother had just come through the door, looking very excited. As Miguel expected, he did not share with him what got him so happy.

- Hey kid, I didn't raie you to not say hi when you come home! he said in a stern tone.

- Hello! Nelson replied cheerfully.

He threw his jacket on a chair, whistling.

- Did your thing go well? muttered Miguel.

He was acting disinterested but it did not seem to bother his brother.

- Mmh yes, it was fine.

- You won?

- Won what?

- Were you chosen?

- Chosen for what?

- Stop acting dumb! You know very well what I mean!

His behaviour was annoying him.

- Yes and if you want to know everything,

everyone loved my song. I blew the audience away! he exclaimed with a smile.

- It's good. You did good, I hope you'll be successful...

- What does that mean? Nelson said, frowning.

- That means it's not people's approval that's going to pay the bills.

- Money, money! That's the only thing that matters to you! For me, it's my voice it's authentic, real! Your money brings you nothing but trouble!

- And food on the table! Without me, you would be left eating your shit! If your success depends on a favour, you remain indebted and dependent on your master! Let me tell you a story bro. Take a pane of glass, on one side there is a bird and on the other side there is a fly. The fly constantly bumps into the window to find a way out. The bird bangs its head twice trying to catch the fly. And then he understands and flies away to other projects. The fly will continue to bang against the same window until it dies! Are you a fly or a fucking bird?

- You know what Miguel, fuck you! I didn't ask

for your opinion anyway.

Nelson climbed the stairs four steps at a time and slammed his bedroom door shut behind him. Shit, thought Miguel. I'm too fucking dumb! He banged his fist on the table. He was not great at talking, he was better when he let his fists do the talking. Once again, it showed the gulf that separated them. He regretted his words, as he always did after their arguments. Deep down, he would rather see Nelson locked in his room with his music than hanging out in the street and getting arrested by the cops. The young man took a deep breath and ran his hand through his hair. Tonight, instead of arguing with his brother, he was going to make it up to him and congratulate him. He climbed the stairs following his brother, going over each word he was going to say. He knocked on the door.

- Go away.

He opened the door anyway and was met with glaring eyes.

- I am sorry. I didn't want to ruin your evening, he said, approaching the bed.

- As usual…

- I'm sorry if I didn't come to see your performance but I'm sure you shut them all up and I'm very proud of you.

Nelson finally deigned looking up from his music book when he heard those words. His brother was never sorry, especially when he was wrong and the fact that he was proud of him felt good.

- You have to be drunk or stoned to say that, Nelson said, arching an eyebrow.

- Why do you say that? I only had a beer. No, in all seriousness, I'm happy for you, even if it doesn't pay the bills right now, I'm sure someday, it will.

They exchanged an intimate smile.

- You know what? You and your girl are invited to the party I'm throwing at the night club; you can bring other friends from your school if you want too. You guys will have a great time, it's an open bar!

- She's not my girl, her name is Ana, Nelson

retorted, patting his brother's shoulder softly. But yeah, with pleasure!

The two brothers had finally found common ground, everyone was happy. Even if they had grown up and had their own grown up problems, they remained brothers and that, they had ended up forgetting it.

- Tell me bro, there's something that's been bugging me for years, why do you always dress the same?

- Just so I can have an asshole asking me that very question…

They laughed like had not laughed for a very long time.

CHAPTER 10

As soon as music class was over, Nelson invited Ana and Veronica to Miguel's party. The reason he was inviting Veronica was that he was hoping she would befriend his brother. Veronica had told him she really liked him. He, himself was hoping to make things official with Ana, even if Jorge was always lurking. Deep down, he was certain his feelings were reciprocated, especially after she had kissed his cheek that last time. It was only a few more days before the party, and he could not wait.

At school, Ana and Veronica were also very excited about the party. Jorge was suspiciously watching them, asking them lots of questions. He was very intrigued by their whispering but the two young women were not revealing much to him. Ana certainly did not want him to invite himself, especially since that was his style. This situation was driving him crazy, Ana was driving him crazy. This little bitch would be his, even if he had to force himself on her. He was convinced that she had fallen in love with this freaking black man and that he was the one responsible for the invitation, which he considered foolish. He tried everything to prevent Ana from going by suggesting her other plans for the evening. But it was a lost battle, the young girl acted as if she was already there. Lucky for him, Jorge had a plan B…

Night Club, 10:30 p.m.

The party was in full swing; everyone was dancing wildly to the music. Strobe lights were illuminating the dance floor. Ana and Nelson had managed to find one another in the crowd and were not leaving each other's side. The booze and the party's mood had brought them even closer together and they were now flirting like two teenagers at prom. Ana was more beautiful than ever, she was smiling and letting herself be free like she had not done in a long time. Nelson was happy to see her like this, he was with his beloved, his friends and his brother with whom he was close once again. They were laughing out loud, no longer caring about real life or the world outside. Sometimes they kissed, sometimes they touched. One thing was certain, they loved each other deeply and had hidden it for far too long.

Meanwhile, Veronica had her heart set on Miguel, but he was busy doing business. He did not trust the people surrounding him. He was watching out for the tiniest movement, the slightest anomaly, without seeing the young woman's desperate attempts. She thought it was a game without realizing her life could turn into a tragedy in a split second. But it was not her fault, she ignored everything about Miguel's way of life, she only saw the picture he presented to society, the face a young successful entrepreneur. Finally, the young man relaxed a little and offered himself a moment of leisure with the young woman; after all, her company was not that unpleasant.

Not far away, Jorge was lurking in the shadows, a glass of whiskey in his hand. He was keeping an attentive aye on the two lovers and was slowly becoming annoyed. They had isolated themselves and spent their time kissing. He was dying to step in to separate them, to kill Nelson, to take back his girlfriend, but it was too risky. His freaky brother was a real sentinel; he was on the lookout for the slightest suspicious person. It was easy enough to notice as he had been watching over the club the whole night. So Jorge was left just sitting there, watching them, cursing them, planning his revenge until he could not take it anymore and left the party.

CHAPTER 11

Ana went home with Nelson. The two lovebirds did not leave each other's sides and were spending all their free time in bed, intertwined, whispering sweet nothings to each other. It was the first time that the young girl saw the place where her boyfriend lived, a small, cold, rather dull house. Surprisingly, she still felt at home there and did not regret her boring life as a lonely princess. For Nelson, she was ready to live anywhere and make any sacrifices. Without understanding how or why, she was certain he was this man she would grow old with. She had forgotten all about her father and Jorge, and how their toxic behaviour was making her more miserable, week after week. At last, she felt herself coming back to life and getting back to her former herself again. As for Nelson, he was the happiest man in the world, he finally had the relationship he had been dreaming about with Ana. The more he looked at her, the more his love for her grew. He covered her with kisses and caresses, complimented her but also teased her a little. They were lovers but also friends and that only strengthened their relationship. All he wanted for his life was for her to be right next to him and for them to support each other. They were both in their twenties and they just had to make their way. During pillow talks, future projects were formed, their imagination and their desire knowing no limits. They already pictured themselves home, in a beautiful house that would be theirs, their children, happy and fulfilled. After all, that is all that truly matters, being a family with the person you love the most in the world. Each of them succeeding in their professional career, being fulfilled. They were giddy with excitement between the sheets of Nelson's tiny bed. The latter made a promise to Ana, the most beautiful of all. He promised her fidelity, support and love. He swore to her that he would not let anyone separate them. Even though it was very cliché and said under the influence of emotion, Ana chose to believe him with all her heart because his promise was filled with hope and kindness.

During the following weeks, the lovebirds spent their free time together. Sometimes at Nelson's, when Miguel was away, and sometimes at Ana's, when her father was away. They lived on love and fresh water and more often than not found themselves between the sheets. They hid as best they could but Veronica knew what was going on between them and as a faithful friend she kept their secret. Jorge suspected something, but Ana played the silent card as soon as he started asking questions. She prayed every day that he would eventually give up. But he was not backing off and each day his questions were more and more detailed, more precise as if he already knew the answers to them. Even Miguel, who only saw them occasionally, had quickly understood what was going on between the two of them and had taken up the annoying habit of teasing his little brother about it. Fortunately, Nelson had some tricks up his sleeve himself and was quick to ask Miguel in return about his supposedly secret relationship with Veronica. They laughed about it, and it was a joyous time.

It seemed like everything was going smoothly but in the shadows, Jorge was waiting for the right moment to strike. One day, he decided to put an end to this romantic comedy. At the end of a school day, Ana was about leaving to meet up with Nelson. She waved her friends goodbye and started walking away. Jorge was not far and was watching her every move. He rushed to her to start an argument in front of the other students. As the tone rose, Jorge was getting increasingly aggressive both verbally and physically. He was being menacing, pushing her and mistreating her. He threatened to go tell her father about her unnatural relationship with Nelson, whom he called a dirty nigger, promising that he would do everything to make her life miserable.

- What would your mother think? You're

behaving like a whore! She would be ashamed of you, she must be turning in her grave as we speak, the poor thing!

These words deeply hurt the young woman. Jorge had just revealed his true face which was an elaborate mix of stupidity and absolute evil. Veronica was not far away and watched the scene unfold. She immediately came to her friend's rescue. She shoved Jorge away, calling him an asshole, and Jorge ended up leaving, still spewing insults at her.

- Ana, how are you? asked the young woman, worried.

These words triggered a wave of sobs and tremors in Ana. Veronica hugged her and pulled her away from prying eyes. As the young girl came to her senses and calmed down, a strong fit of nausea seized her. Veronica barely had time to pull away before her friend vomited her lunch on the floor.

- It's okay, said Veronica. It's the emotion, it's going to be fine.

She gently stroked Ana's back. But the latter

was not so sure that Jorge was the true cause of this inconvenience, he had only just induced it. She put her hand over her mouth and started shaking.

- Oh Veronica… I think I'm pregnant…

CHAPTER 12

Jorge was furious. He was terribly angry with Ana for choosing this failure, this measly Nelson over him. It was beyond him; he didn't understand what he had done to deserve this. He had always loved Ana. He had put her on a pedestal and dedicated his whole life to her. He had showered her with gifts and love, had given her his full attention but it still had not been enough. She was like everyone else, perpetually unsatisfied and she had broken his heart, without thinking twice about it. He still had a trick up his sleeve to make her pay for what she had done to him. He revved up his sports sedan's engine and made it to Ana's within minutes. After their violent argument, she must have taken refuge with her lover and Jorge had the house all to himself. Paolo was there as he expected. Jorge put on his face his most depressed look and went inside the house. He told Ana's father everything, sobbing. He told him about Nelson, that Negro friend of hers, who had finally become his daughter's lover. It did not take long for Paolo to burst with rage, as Jorge stirred up his anger, explaining how Nelson got hold of drugs and gave them to Ana. He also told him that she attended his brother's orgies and then hung out in the suburbs surrounded by prostitutes. Paolo could not warp his head around it; how could his little girl have done this to him? She, for whom he overworked himself to offer her the best future, he had even planned to appoint her as deputy director of his company as soon as she had finished her studies! And how could she have left poor Jorge, such a good boy with such a promising future? He could not believe his ears! He comforted the boy and told him to go back home, assuring him that he would take care of setting Ana straight, starting tonight, without suspecting that he there was still some things he ignored.

Ana was expecting a baby; the pregnancy tests she had taken had confirmed her fear. She was panicking, did not know what to do, it was a complete disaster! She exited the school bathroom and decided to go home to find comfort in her father. She was not sure how he would react but she had no other choice at the moment. She was afraid that if she told Nelson, he would run away and dump her as soon as she said the word "baby". She was ashamed of herself, how had could she have forgotten protection? Such recklessness, such carelessness. One thing was certain, her father would not fail to remind her of that. Pill or condoms, she had not even thought about them for a second. Neither did Nelson. The more she thought about it, the more she worried about the consequences. Should she keep the baby? Should she abort? All the solutions seemed terrible. She arrived home, her father was waiting for her, sitting in the dining room, looking serious. Ana knew this attitude and suspected that he knew something. She greeted him shyly, he nodded and glared at her.

- You have nothing to say to me?

- What? Ana answered hesitantly.

- You know what I'm talking about Ana!

Her father could not know, it was impossible.

- Dad, what are you talking about?

- About your relationship with your little nigger!

- His name is Nelson, Dad. And I do what I want!

- No, you don't do what you want, you're my daughter, you live in my house and 'm the one putting food on the table! To think, I trusted you while you're getting high on the street with those dirty guys! You make me ashamed Ana, fortunately your mother is no longer there to see that!

- You have no right to say that…, sobbed the young girl.

- I do have the right, your mother wanted the best for you and look at what you're doing, look at what you became! The laughingstock of the family, a good for nothing drug addict! But from today on, you won't see this nigger anymore, it's over! You are locked up in your room until I decide otherwise. You are only allowed outside to go to school and Jorge will be the one picking you up and driving you back. Music lessons are over!

- You have no right to do that dad! I am not a minor anymore, I am free to go wherever I want, whenever I want and with whomever I want! I refuse to be locked up in this horrible house where I am alone all the time! And you know what? Since you love Nelson so much, you will be delighted to learn that I am expecting his baby!

That was it, the truth was out. Ana thought her father would be understanding and caring, but he acted like a real bully. And she was convinced that he had been told everything by Jorge.

- What?! exclaimed Paolo, angry like he had never been before. You are pregnant? That dirty nigger did that to you?

- Yes dad and whether you like it or not, I'm going to keep this child. Whatever you think of Nelson, he's a good person, he's better than both you and Jorge. He makes me happy and I'd rather be with him than here with you.

Ana had made her decision. This child was his, it was the fruit of her love with Nelson, the best thing that had happened to her in life. And as they had promised each other, no one and nothing could separate them.

- There's no way you're carrying this abomination! Go up to your room now! I will call a doctor. And give me your phone!

- No! It's my child, it's my body, I'm the one who gets to decide. You didn't listen to anything! You never listen! You never paid attention to mom either!

- In your bedroom, now! He ordered, pointing to the stairs.

- No!

- If you don't obey, you can say goodbye to me and to everything else. I will write you off my will and you will never be a part of this family ever again. I'm ashamed of you, there's no way you're raising this kid here. If you decide to leave, get out but you won't be my daughter anymore!

- Okay dad, it's goodbye then, Ana replied sobbing, okay. By the way, mom spent her whole life loving you but you only ever loved yourself. So I wish you all the happiness in the world...

She walked away without looking back. Her own father saying those kind of words was excruciating. If he really loved her, he would never have reacted like that. She grabbed her phone to call Nelson. He was her last hope. After a few rings, he finally picked up. Ana told him everything, that Jorge had told her father about their relationship, that he had just kicked her out of her house. She pondered for a second and finally told him about the baby she was expecting. Nelson was surprised but the surprise quickly turned into joy for the young girl's delight and relief

- Sweetie, go to Veronica's, I'll finish my delivery promptly and I'll join you as soon as possible. I love you.

Nelson hung up. He had agreed to help out Tonio one last time while he found a new delivery man and it was very bad timing. He hurried to make the delivery, the customer's address was not very far away. He could only think only of Ana and the baby, their baby. He had not thought for a second that he could have impregnated Ana while they were having sex. But it had happened and it was not the end of the world, they would get through it. But the fact that her father kicked her out because of him, that he could not believe. It was all Jorge's fault! But his priority now was to take care of Ana, he would plot his revenge later.

CHAPTER 13

As Nelson raced through the streets of Lisbon to meet up with his girlfriend, he had not noticed that Jorge was following him, waiting for the right opportunity to strike. The young boy finally reached his last delivery. Even though it was not very professional of him, he was being hasty and rapidly got back on his scooter afterwards. Suddenly, a car sped up, coming up towards him at full speed. He jumped off his scooter, the car missing him by only an inch. The car was already speeding away. The driver was fleeing the scene and Nelson was determined to go after him. He was not sure but he thought he had recognized Jorge in the rear view mirror and that meant it was not a mere accident but rather an attempted murder. Nelson lifted up his scooter. It was slightly damaged but still worked. He restarted the engine and sped after the fleeing driver. He found him a few blocks away, stopped at a red light. Nelson got off his scooter to confront the man, it was indeed Jorge who was responsible for the criminal attempt Nelson just experienced. He had wanted to get revenge on Jorge, and that was the perfect opportunity to do so. Nelson opened the passenger door and forced Jorge out, pulling him by his jacket's collar.

- If you don't let it go, I'll destroy you!

- What are you talking about?

His smirk was proof enough that he was guilty.

- You bastard! Nelson was manhandling him. If there were no witnesses, I would kill you!

Suddenly, he could hear police sirens behind him. A police car pulled up next to them and two police officers got out, carrying handcuffs and truncheons.

- Shit! Nelson exclaimed, letting go of Jorge.

- Sucks to be you, Jorge whispered, sounding satisfied. You will go back to your cage.

They took Nelson away without really knowing what had actually happened. A blue butterfly twirled around Nelson's leg, and without meaning to, he accidently smashed it... When they arrived at the police station, the young boy experienced the police's blatant racism. Although he was itching to talk back, he remained calm much to the officers' disappointment. According to the policemen, he was going to spend the night in custody and would be tried the very next day, in an immediate appearance. Thanks to his legal right to one phone call, he could contact one person and he chose his older brother. He was the only one who could help him in this situation. Miguel answered and Nelson told him everything, starting from the beginning. The young man was very worried about Ana, whom he had left alone, and he hoped she had safely made it to Veronica's. He was afraid that Jorge had found her and had taken her back to her father to have a forced abortion. Miguel promised his little brother that he would pick him up at the police station within the next hour. Nelson had no choice but to believe him and he hung up. Although Miguel was very eager to make this Jorge guy pay, family came first. First, he called Veronica to make sure Ana was there and she confirmed it. He briefly let her know about his brother's misadventure and hung up. Without further ado, he took his belongings and left the party he was at. But as he was about to get into his car, a shadow passed behind him and hit him on the head, hard. Miguel fell to the ground, unconscious. Before losing consciousness, he recognized the club's owner who had tried to scam him a few weeks before and an acquaintance of his, Pablo, another party promoter and former friend.

- There boss, one less problem! And don't worry, I'll be taking care of the parties from now on and they'll be much better than his.

Miguel had noticed some strange things happening around him, but had not been suspicious of Pablo. They left him lying in the parking lot, his head cracked open. A few minutes later, a young woman found Miguel injured and unconscious. She immediately called for an ambulance. They took the young man to the hospital giving him first aid, but he was in very poor shape.

CHAPTER 14

After having spent the worst night of his life, Nelson struggled to wake up. He had been having nightmares for the past eight hours, thinking the worst had happened to Ana and his brother. Now more than ever, he felt truly alone. In a few minutes, he was going to be judged for a crime he did not commit. He did not deserve to be here but he had to control his anger, so as not to aggravate his case. He was still entitled to a breakfast that looked a lot like dog food. The young man was far too stressed to eat it anyway. He was pacing in his cell. He just wanted to find Ana and make sure she and the baby were safe. Then he would go get revenge on Jorge, for real this time. That bastard had been very lucky yesterday but he would not get that much luck twice.

An officer appeared and told Nelson that the hearing would begin shortly. He took him out of his cell in handcuffs. The young man did not even have a lawyer, he would surely be appointed one. He did not think he needed one anyway as he had not done anything wrong. As he entered the court, the young man kept his head held high and prayed that the judge would not be a racist as well. The following hour would shape the rest of his life.

An hour later Nelson was walking away, a free man. He had been lucky in his misfortune, an eyewitness had seen Jorge trying to run him over and had spontaneously come to plead his case. Without him, Nelson would have been charged with physical assault and sentenced to six months in prison. The officers who had arrested him the day before reluctantly gave him back his belongings. No sooner was he outside the police station than he immediately called Ana. She had tried to call him about twenty times and he was terribly sorry for not having been there for her. Unfortunately, she did not pick up. He hoped she was not mad at him. He decided to go home to pick up some things. On his way, he tried to call his brother but he did not answer any of his calls either. He was starting to seriously worry. As Nelson was approaching his home, Nico, one of his brother's friends called out for him. His facial expressions did not bode well.

- Nel! Hold on! We looked for you everywhere all night long, where were you? he said, distraught.

- In jail, why? What is happening?

- It's your brother, he's in the hospital, he's in a coma...

A shiver ran down his spine. Miguel? In a hospital? In a coma? He did not let Nico say another word and stormed off to the hospital. On the drive there, he was imagining the worst. He tried to reach Ana but she still was not picking up. Too bad, he had to see his brother. As he pulled into the emergency parking lot, his phone finally rang but it was not Ana. He picked it up, it was the

Professor.

- Nelson, my boy, how are you? he said in a delighted tone.

- Professor… I can't talk to you right now, I…

The old gentleman interrupted him.

- Nelson, I have good news for you: one of my good friends, Fernando, offered to become your producer. He loved you at the annual performance! He wants to meet you tomorrow at school. This is a fantastic opportunity!

Nelson felt like a deer in headlights. He accepted the Professor's offer and hung up. Behind him, a car pulled up, tires loudly screeching. The young man turned around briskly fearing that Jorge had come back to finish him off. Then he recognized the lovely golden hair of his girlfriend who was walking towards him accompanied by Veronica. Ana threw herself into his arms.

- I was so scared...

Nelson reassured her and asked them what they were doing here. Nico had called Veronica to tell her about Miguel's situation and she had come running here. The trio immediately rushed into the hospital in search of Miguel. As Nico had said, he was in a coma. The doctor explained to them what had happened and Veronica burst into tears. His chances of survival were slim. Nelson remained silent, still in shock. He knew that his brother lived a dangerous life but he never thought he would be victim of an assassination attempt. He went back to his brother's hospital room where he was peacefully sleeping. The numerous machines' incessant beeping punctuated his pulse. Nelson sat down next to him and took his hand. At the touch of his cold hand, his shoulders sagged. If Miguel died, there would be no one of his family left and he refused to lose him when they had only just reconciled. Suddenly, a piercing shrill sound ringed in Nelson's ears. He did not have time to understand what was happening as three doctors rushed into the room. They told him to leave the room and started doing resuscitation manoeuvres. His face glued to the room's window, Nelson felt paralyzed and totally helpless.

Ten minutes later, one of the doctors announced the news: the young man had not survived.

EPILOGUE

12 months later

Like every Friday night, a performance is taking place in the prestigious hall of the Atlantic Pavilion in Lisbon. In the kind of place where only people from the upper class have the opportunity to come and admire great artists performing on stage. To secure a good seat, you had to book it two months in advance and tonight is special. Today the Atlantic Pavilion in Lisbon is welcoming a new artist and everyone is eager to meet him. He will undoubtedly sell out the room for several months and everyone wants to be in the front row to listen to him and admire him. At 9 p.m., the crowd hurries up next the building's gates. Only people with an invitation can enter. It is an indescribable stampede.

The performance starts in half an hour and the hall is already packed. In the middle of the front row a radiant young woman with shiny hair is sitting. Her name is Anna. Of all the people in the room, she is surely the happiest to be here. She has been waiting for this moment for months and it is finally here. Around her, people whisper and ask questions about this new artist who will dazzle them. The impatience is at its height. She smiles mischievously, she will be the only one not to be surprised when the curtain rises because she knows the artist who lives in her heart.

Finally, the lights slowly dim, turning the room dark. People fall silent and hold their breath. The curtain rises and reveals a man in his twenties, smiling with bright eyes, maybe tearful. Tonight, the artist that the crowd applauds is Nelson, Fado's revelation. His gaze travels to the front row, his wife in a magnificent blue dress is smiling at him, and his brother Miguel is at her side... Tonight is his moment of glory, the one he has been waiting for all his life.

FSC
www.fsc.org
MIXTE
Papier issu
de sources
responsables
Paper from
responsible sources
FSC® C105338